HORRiD HENRY'S
Nits

HORRID HENRY'S
Nits

Francesca Simon
Illustrated by Tony Ross

Orion
Children's Books

Horrid Henry's Nits originally appeared in
Horrid Henry's Nits first published in Great Britain
in 1997 by Orion Children's Books
This edition first published in Great Britain in 2010
by Orion Children's Books
a division of the Orion Publishing Group Ltd
Orion House
5 Upper Saint Martin's Lane
London WC2H 9EA
An Hachette UK Company

1 3 5 7 9 10 8 6 4 2

The Orion Publishing Group's policy is to use papers that
are natural, renewable and recyclable products and made
from wood grown in sustainable forests. The logging and
manufacturing processes are expected to conform to the
environmental regulations of the country of origin.

A catalogue record for this book is available from the British Library.

ISBN 978 1 4440 0100 6

Printed and bound in China

www.orionbooks.co.uk
www.horridhenry.co.uk

This book is dedicated to William Gee who would like to thank all the boys in 2BC at The Hall School for being such great classmates:

Laurie Ashcroft
Gus Beagles
Angus Bloch
James Claydon
Nicholas Corbett
Luke Eadie
Alec Ezra
Max Fairfull
Jacob Goldberg
Cal Gorvy
Thomas Hocking
Boaz Lister
Phelim Owens
Tej Shah
Zaki Siddiqui
Nathaniel Swift
James Taylor

We would also like to thank the following teachers: Rebecca McDonald, Susie Wesson, Nicky Gill, Kirsty Anderson and of course Katie Bonham-Carter.

Look out for . . .

Contents

Chapter 1

Scratch. Scratch. Scratch.

Dad scratched his head.
"Stop scratching, please," said Mum.
"We're eating dinner."

Mum scratched her head.
"Stop scratching, please," said Dad.
"We're eating dinner."

Henry scratched his head.

"Stop scratching, Henry!"
said Mum and Dad.

"Uh-oh," said Mum. She put down
her fork and frowned at Henry.
"Henry, do you have nits *again*?"

"Of course not," said Henry.

"Come over to the sink, Henry,"
said Mum.

"Why?" said Henry.

"I need to check your head."

Henry dragged his feet over to her
as slowly as possible. It's not fair,
he thought.

It wasn't his fault nits loved him.
Henry's head was a gathering place
for nits far and wide. They probably
held nit parties there and foreign nits
visited him on their holidays.

Mum dragged the nit comb across
Henry's head. She made a face
and groaned.
"You're crawling with nits, Henry,"
said Mum.

"Ooh, let's see," said Henry.
He always liked counting
how many nits he had.

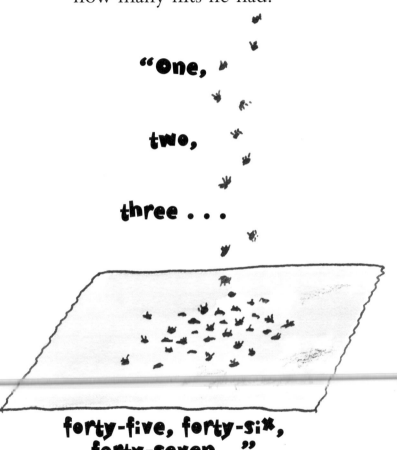

"One,

two,

three . . .

forty-five, forty-six,
forty-seven..."

he counted, dropping them
on to a paper towel.

"It's not polite to count nits,"
said his younger brother,
Perfect Peter, wiping his mouth
with his spotless napkin.
"Is it, Mum?"

"It certainly isn't," said Mum.

Chapter 2

Dad dragged the nit comb across
his head and made a face.
"Ughh," said Dad.

Mum dragged the comb through
her hair.
"Bleccch," said Mum.

Mum combed Perfect Peter's hair.
Then she did it again. And again.
And again.

"No nits, Peter," said Mum, smiling.
"As usual. Well done, darling."
Perfect Peter smiled modestly.
"It's because I wash and comb my
hair every night," said Peter.

Henry scowled. True, his hair was
filthy, but then . . .
"Nits love clean hair," said Henry.

"No they don't," said Peter.
"*I've* never ever had nits."

We'll see about that, thought Henry.

When no one was looking he picked
a few nits off the paper towel.
Then he wandered over to Peter and
casually fingered a lock of his hair.

LEAP!

Scratch.

Scratch.

"Mum!" squealed Peter. "Henry's
pulling my hair!"

"Stop it, Henry," said Dad.

"I wasn't pulling his hair,"
said Henry indignantly.
"I just wanted to see how clean
it was. And it *is* so lovely and clean,"
added Henry sweetly.

"I wish my hair was as clean as Peter's."
Peter beamed. It wasn't often that
Henry said anything nice to him.

"Right," said Mum grimly, "everyone upstairs. It's shampoo time."

Chapter 3

"NO!" shrieked Horrid Henry.

He hated the stinky smelly horrible shampoo much more than he hated having nits. Only today his teacher, Miss Battle-Axe, had sent home a nit letter.

BEWARE!

Nits Nits Nits Nits

Nits have been seen in school.

GET RID OF THEM!

**Wash your hair with supersonic
NIT Blasting Shampoo**

PLEASE ...

OR ELSE.

Naturally, Henry had crumpled
the letter and thrown it away.
He was never ever going to have
pongy nit shampoo on his head
again. What rotten luck Mum had
spotted him scratching.

"It's the only way to get rid
of nits," said Dad.

"But it never works!" screamed
Henry. And he ran for the door.
Mum and Dad grabbed him.
Then they dragged him kicking
and screaming to the bathroom.

"Nits are living creatures,"
howled Henry. "Why kill them?"

"Because..." said Mum.

"Because ... because ... they're
blood-sucking nits," said Dad.

Blood-sucking.

Henry had never thought of that.

In the split second that he stood
still to consider this interesting
information, Mum emptied the
bottle of supersonic nit–blasting
shampoo over his hair.
"NO!" screamed Henry.
Frantically he shook his head.

There was shampoo on the door.
There was shampoo on the floor.
There was shampoo all over
Mum and Dad.
The only place there was
no shampoo was on Henry's head.
"Henry! Stop being horrid!" yelled
Dad, wiping shampoo off his jacket.

"What a big fuss over nothing,"
said Peter.
Henry lunged at him.
Mum seized Henry by the collar
and held him back.

"Now, Peter," said Mum. "That wasn't
a kind thing to say to Henry, was it?
Not everyone is as brave as you."

"You're right, Mum," said Perfect Peter. "I was being rude and thoughtless. It won't happen again. I'm so sorry, Henry."

Mum smiled at him. "That was a perfect apology, Peter. As for you, Henry . . ." she sighed. "We'll get more shampoo tomorrow."

Phew, thought Henry, giving his head an extra good scratch. Safe for one more day.

Chapter 4

The next morning at school a group
of parents burst into the classroom,
waving the nit letter and shouting.

My Margaret doesn't have nits! She never has and she never will. How dare you send home such a letter!

shrieked Moody Margaret's mother.

The idea! My Josh doesn't have nits,

shouted his mother.

My Toby doesn't have nits! Some nasty child in this class isn't bug-busting!

shouted his father.

Miss Battle-Axe squared her
shoulders.
"Rest assured that the culprit
will be found," she said.
"I have declared war on nits."

Scratch. Scratch. Scratch.

Miss Battle-Axe spun round.
Her beady eyes swivelled
over the class.
"Who's scratching?" she demanded.

Silence.

Henry bent over his worksheet and
tried to look studious.
"Henry is," said Moody Margaret.

"Liar!" shouted Horrid Henry.
"It was William!"
Weepy William burst into tears.
"No it wasn't," he sobbed.

Miss Battle-Axe glared at the class. "I'm going to find out once and for all who's got nits," she growled.

"Silence!" ordered Miss Battle-Axe. "Nora, the nit nurse, is coming this morning. Who's got nits? Who's not bug-busting? We'll all find out soon."

Uh-oh, thought Henry.
Now I'm sunk.

There was no escaping Nitty Nora
Bug Explorer and her ferocious
combs. **Everyone** would know
he had the nits.

Rude Ralph would never
stop teasing him.

He'd be shampooed every night.

Mum and Dad would find out
about all the nit letters he'd
thrown away . . .

He could of course get a tummy
ache double quick and be sent home.
But Nitty Nora had a horrible way
of remembering whose head she
hadn't checked and then combing
it in front of the whole class.

He could run screaming out of the
door saying he'd caught mad cow
disease. But somehow he didn't think
Miss Battle-Axe would believe him.
There was no way out. This time
he was well and truly stuck.

Unless . . .
Suddenly Henry had a wonderful,
spectacular idea.

It was so wicked, and so horrible,
that even Horrid Henry hesitated.

But only for a moment.
Desperate times call for desperate
measures.

Chapter 5

Henry leaned over Clever Clare and
brushed his head lightly against hers.

LEAP!

Scratch.

Scratch.

"Get away from me, Henry,"
hissed Clare.
"I was just admiring your lovely
picture," said Henry.

He got up to sharpen his pencil.
On his way to the sharpener he
brushed against Greedy Graham.

LEAP!

Scratch. Scratch.

On his way back from the sharpener
Henry stumbled and fell against
Anxious Andrew.

LEAP!

Scratch.

Scratch.

"Ow!" yelped Andrew.
"Sorry, Andrew," said Henry.
"What big clumsy feet I have."

"Whoops!" he added, tripping over
the carpet and banging heads
with Weepy William.

LEAP!

Scratch.

Scratch.

"Waaaaaaaaa!" wailed William.
"Sit down at once, Henry,"
said Miss Battle-Axe.
"William! Stop scratching.
Bert! How do you spell cat?"

"I dunno," said Beefy Bert.
Horrid Henry leaned across the table
and put his head close to Bert's.
"C-A-T," he whispered helpfully.

Then Horrid Henry raised his hand.
"Yes?" said Miss Battle-Axe.
"I don't understand these
instructions," said Henry sweetly.
"Could you help me, please?"

Miss Battle-Axe frowned.
She liked to keep as far away from
Henry as possible. Reluctantly she
came closer and bent over his work.

Henry leaned his head near hers.

LEAP!

Scratch.

Scratch.

Chapter 6

There was a pounding at the door. Then Nitty Nora marched into the classroom, bristling with combs and other instruments of torture.

"Line up, everyone,"
said Miss Battle-Axe, patting her hair.
"The nit nurse is here."

Rats, thought Henry.
He'd hardly started.
Slowly, he stood up.

Everyone pushed and shoved to be
first in line. Then a few children
remembered what they were
lining up for and stampeded
towards the back.

Horrid Henry saw his chance
and took it.
He charged through the squabbling
children, brushing against everyone
as fast as he could.

LEAP!

 Scratch! Scratch!

 # LEAP!

Scratch!

Scratch!

 # LEAP!

Scratch!

Scratch!

"Henry!" shouted Miss Battle-Axe.
"Stay in at playtime. Now go to the
end of the queue. The rest if you,
stop this nonsense at once!"

58

Moody Margaret had fought longest and hardest to be first. Proudly she presented her head to Nitty Nora. "I certainly don't have nits," she said.

Nitty Nora stuck the comb in.

"Nits!"

she announced, stuffing a nit note
into Margaret's hand.
For once Margaret was too shocked
to speak.

"But . . . but . . ." she gasped.

Tee-hee, thought Henry.
Now he wouldn't be the only one.

"Next," said Nitty Nora.
She stuck the comb in
Rude Ralph's greasy hair.

"Nits!" she announced.

"Nit-face," hissed Horrid Henry,
beside himself with glee.

"Nits!" said Nitty Nora, poking her comb into Lazy Linda's mop.

"Nits!"

said Nitty Nora, prodding Greedy Graham's frizzy hair.

"Nits, nits, nits, nits, nits!"

she continued, pointing at Weepy William, Clever Clare, Sour Susan, Beefy Bert and Dizzy Dave.

Then Nitty Nora beckoned to
Miss Battle-Axe.
"Teachers too," she ordered.

Miss Battle-Axe's jaw dropped.
"I have been teaching for twenty-five
years and I have never had nits,"
she said. "Don't waste your time
checking *me*."

Nitty Nora ignored her protests
and stuck in the comb.
"Hmmn," she said, and whispered
in Miss Battle-Axe's ear.

"NO!"

howled Miss Battle-Axe.

"NOOOOOOOOOO!"

Then she joined the line of
weeping, wailing children clutching
their nit notes.

At last it was Henry's turn.
Nitty Nora stuck her comb into
Henry's tangled hair and dragged it
across his scalp. She combed again.
And again. And again.

"No nits," said Nitty Nora.
"Keep up the good work,
young man."
"I sure will!" said Henry.

Horrid Henry skipped home
waving his certificate.
"Look, Peter," crowed Henry.
"I'm nit-free!"
Perfect Peter burst into tears.
"I'm not," he wailed.

"Hard luck," said Horrid Henry.

More HORRiD HENRY

Horrid Henry
Horrid Henry and the Secret Club
Horrid Henry Tricks the Tooth Fairy
Horrid Henry's Nits
Horrid Henry Gets Rich Quick
Horrid Henry's Haunted House
Horrid Henry and the Mummy's Curse
Horrid Henry's Revenge
Horrid Henry and the Bogey Babysitter
Horrid Henry's Stinkbomb
Horrid Henry's Underpants
Horrid Henry Meets the Queen
Horrid Henry and the Mega-Mean Time Machine
Horrid Henry and the Football Fiend
Horrid Henry's Christmas Cracker
Horrid Henry and the Abominable Snowman
Horrid Henry Robs the Bank
Horrid Henry Wakes the Dead

Horrid Henry's Joke Book
Horrid Henry's Jolly Joke Book
Horrid Henry's Mighty Joke Book
Horrid Henry Versus Moody Margaret

Colour Books

Horrid Henry's Big Bad Book
Horrid Henry's Wicked Ways
Horrid Henry's Evil Enemies
Horrid Henry Rules the World
Horrid Henry's House of Horrors
Horrid Henry's Dreadful Deeds

Activity Books

Horrid Henry's Brainbusters
Horrid Henry's Headscratchers
Horrid Henry's Mindbenders
Horrid Henry's Colouring Book
Horrid Henry's Puzzle Book
Horrid Henry's Sticker Book
Horrid Henry's Mad Mazes
Horrid Henry's Wicked Wordsearches
Horrid Henry's Crazy Crosswords
Horrid Henry's Classroom Chaos
Horrid Henry's Holiday Havoc
Horrid Henry Runs Riot

Early Reader

HORRiD HENRY
and the
Football Fiend

Francesca Simon
Illustrated by Tony Ross

utterly wicked.
Totally brilliant.

Horrid Henry is determined
to win the football match,
whatever it takes.
But Moody Margaret has
other ideas . . .

utterly wicked.
Totally brilliant.

Henry needs money – and fast! But his
skeleton bank is empty, and his parents
won't give him any, so just how is he
going to do it? Then Henry has a
brilliant idea . . .

Utterly wicked.
Totally brilliant.

Henry HATES holidays. He would rather
stay at home and watch TV. But he likes
the idea of a camping trip.
The journey isn't at all what he expects
– and neither is the campsite!
It's going to be a disaster . . .

HORRID HENRY'S *Underpants*

Illustrated by Tony Ross

Francesca Simon

Utterly wicked.

Totally brilliant.

When Henry receives an
unexpected package, he is NOT
impressed to find a hideous pair
of frilly pink pants inside.
He's got to get rid of them –
and quickly!